D1709508

DECADES OF THE 20th AND 21st CENTURIES

The 1930s

Stephen Feinstein

1930s

Stephen Feinstein

Enslow Publishing
101 W. 23rd Street
Suite 240
New York, NY 10011
USA
enslow.com

Published in 2016 by Enslow Publishing, LLC.
101 W. 23rd Street, Suite 240, New York, NY 10011

Library of Congress Cataloging-in-Publication Data
Feinstein, Stephen.
The 1930s / Stephen Feinstein.
    pages cm. — (Decades of the 20th and 21st centuries)
Includes bibliographical references and index.
Summary: "Discusses the decade 1930-1939 in the United States in terms of culture, art, science, and poli-
tics"—Provided by publisher.
Audience: Grade 9 to 12.
ISBN 978-0-7660-6926-8
1. United States—Civilization—1918-1945—Juvenile literature. 2. United States—Politics and govern-
ment—1933-1945—Juvenile literature. 3. United States—Politics and government—1929-1933—Juvenile
literature. 4. Nineteen thirties—Juvenile literature. I. Title.
E169.1.F3549 2015
973.91'6—dc23

                        2015010945

Printed in the United States of America

Photo Credits: Abbie Rowe/PhotoQuest/Getty Images, pp. 29, 88 (top); Arthur Tanner/Fox Photos/Archive
Photos/Getty Images, p. 22; Carl Mydans/The LIFE Images Collection/Getty Images, p. 53; Central Press/
Hulton Archive/Getty Images, pp. 73, 90 (top); Chicago History Museum/Getty Images, p. 78; Cincinnati
Museum Center/Getty Images, p. 40; Courtesy of the National Archives/Newsmakers/Getty Images, pp. 6,
87 (top); DEA/E. GIOVENZANA/De Agostini/Getty Images, p. 83; Everett Historical/Shutterstock.com, p. 3
(bottom right); FPG/Hulton Archive/Getty Images, pp. 35, 45, 46; Franklin D. Roosevelt Presidential Library
& Museum, p. 3 (top left); Haynes Archive/Popperfoto/Getty Images, p. 85; Hulton Archive/Getty Images,
pp. 18, 38, 57, 87 (bottom); Jerry Cooke/Sports Illustrated/Getty Images, p. 43; John Kobal Foundation/
Getty Images, p. 30; Keystone-France/Gamma-Keystone via Getty Images, pp. 3 (top right), 13, 58, 74, 80,
89 (bottom); Library of Congress, Prints & Photographs Division, p. 3 (bottom left); LunaseeStudios/Shut-
terstock.com, pp. 26, 89 (top); Michael Ochs Archives/Getty Images, p. 37; Museum of Science and Industry,
Chicago/Getty Images, p. 14; New York Times Co./Getty Images, p. 49; Peter Stackpole/The LIFE Picture
Collection/Getty Images, p. 50; Photo12/UIG via Getty Images, p. 70; PhotoQuest/Getty Images, pp. 17, 68,
88 (bottom); Popperfoto/Getty Images, pp. 25, 32, 61, 62, 67, 90 (bottom); Transcendental Graphics/Getty
Images, p. 10; Tom Watson/NY Daily News Archive via Getty Images, p. 20; Underwood Archives/Getty Im-
ages, pp. 54, 65; Universal History Archive/UIG via Getty Images, p. 76.

Cover Credits: Everett Historical/Shutterstock.com (soup line); Franklin D. Roosevelt Presidential Library
& Museum (FDR); Keystone-France/Gamma-Keystone via Getty Images (Amelia Earheart); Library of Congress, Prints & Photographs Division (Jesse Owens).

Contents

Herbert Hoover served as president during the Great Depression.

Introduction

The 1930s were a troubled time. America and the world were trapped in the Great Depression. Many people had little or no money. They struggled just to find food. Some families lived in cardboard shacks. It was one of the worst economic crises in history. At the time, few people understood how the Great Depression had happened. Nobody knew when it would end.

The previous decade had been a wild and happy time—the Roaring Twenties. People spent money freely. They fell deep into debt. Their actions were creating unseen problems. The economy was weakening. In 1929, the US stock market crashed. It was the first crisis of the Great Depression. More crises quickly followed. The financial ruin spread across the globe.

At first, President Herbert Hoover did not seem to see how big the problem was. On March 7, 1930, he promised that the Depression would be over in sixty days. Instead, the country sank deeper into the Depression. One by one, businesses failed. The unemployed searched in vain for new jobs. Some sold apples on street corners. Others begged. Families were faced with the threat of starvation. They stood in long lines, hoping to get a free loaf of bread or cup of soup. Banks failed, and many customers lost their life savings.

In 1932, American voters elected a new president, Franklin D. Roosevelt. The fifty-year-old New Yorker was confident. He told Americans that their government had not abandoned them. Roosevelt's efforts would forever change the role of the federal government in the United States.

Unlike Hoover, Roosevelt did not hesitate in taking decisive action to restart the economy. He created a bold plan called the New Deal. Roosevelt constantly talked to the nation on the radio. He spoke in plain words, and his firm voice soothed people's fears. They knew that someone was working hard to help them. Roosevelt always ended his radio talks with a message of encouragement. In short, he gave Americans hope. Americans would reelect Roosevelt four times.

Despite President Roosevelt's efforts, however, the Depression lingered for many years. People grimly went about their lives. They turned to music, movies, and sports to forget about their troubles. They also took pleasure in reading. Newspapers told of heroes, such as the daring female pilot Amelia Earhart. They also reported on outlaws, such as Bonnie and Clyde. The kidnapping of a famous baby in 1932 made headlines. So did the fiery crash of a giant airship in 1937. For fiction, readers looked to cheap magazines called pulps. They also enjoyed the adventures of superheroes. Comic books first became popular in the 1930s.

In other countries, the Great Depression was creating political turmoil. In Germany and Japan, dangerous men used the chaos to strengthen their grip on power. These nations became hostile and warlike. As the 1930s drew to a close, the world plunged toward war. World War II began when Germany invaded Poland on September 1, 1939. It would become the deadliest conflict in human history.

Pop Culture, Lifestyles, and Fashion

In the 1930s, the US economy broke down. This era, known as the Great Depression, came as a sudden and great shock to Americans who had been enjoying the prosperity of the Roaring Twenties.

Breadlines and Soup Kitchens

Every day, millions of Americans in cities and towns all over the country waited patiently in long breadlines at soup kitchens to receive a bowl of soup and some bread. Soup kitchens were the only source of food some people had. In remote locations, such as the mountain towns of Appalachia where there were no soup kitchens, some families survived by eating dandelions and blackberries.

As more people lost their jobs, the breadlines grew longer. Still, some did not admit that something was terribly wrong. President Herbert Hoover kept trying to reassure the nation that everything would be fine. "No one is actually starving," he proclaimed. In the fall of 1930, Hoover created the President's Emergency Committee for Employment (PECE). It did little beyond issuing misleading reports about the adequacy of local relief efforts. Hoover, a self-made millionaire, sincerely believed that any further government attempts to fix what he saw as a "temporary setback" in the economy would only hurt

Americans waited in line for hours for a bowl of soup and piece of bread.

America's greatness. He and others like him believed America was built on hard work, honesty, and the independence of the individual.

By May 1931, however, Hoover could no longer ignore the crisis. Still, he did not want the federal government to lend a helping hand. Hoover thought government charity would rob people of the motivation to take care of themselves. "The way to the nation's greatness is the path of self-reliance," he said. He called for acts of charity by individuals and private enterprise to solve the nation's problems. One citizen who heeded Hoover's request was gangster Al "Scarface" Capone, who set up a soup kitchen in Chicago.

Solutions to Homelessness

Hundreds of thousands of Americans suddenly found themselves homeless. They drifted into a nomadic way of life. They took to riding the rails and hopping freight trains in search of better opportunities in the next town or state. Almost a quarter of a million of these people were teenagers who had become transients when their schools shut down. The number of people on the move was staggering. Officials of the Southern Pacific Railroad claimed to have thrown almost seven hundred thousand rail riders off their trains in just one year!

Meanwhile, thousands of other homeless Americans chose to stay in their hometowns. They slept in doorways, on park benches, underneath bridges, or in abandoned cars. Many went to the outskirts of town where they created communities of shanties. They built shelters out of any available material, such as cardboard or scraps of wood. These communities of the homeless came to be called Hoovervilles. The nickname showed the growing anger at the Hoover administration's failure to take action to solve the nation's problems.

The Mystery of Amelia Earhart

While millions of Americans during the 1930s were spiraling downward, Amelia Earhart was soaring skyward. She had learned to fly in 1920 and quickly developed a passion for it. In 1928, Earhart was a passenger on a flight across the Atlantic Ocean. Then in 1932, she became the first woman to fly solo across the Atlantic when she made the trip from Harbor Grace, Newfoundland, to Ireland in fifteen and a half hours.

Earhart continued to set new records in the sky, twice breaking the women's speed record for a flight from Los Angeles to New York. In 1935, she flew from Hawaii to California, and she was the first person ever to make such a flight. She also helped design airplanes and wrote books about her many adventures.

In 1937, Earhart planned to fly around the world. Other pilots had circled the globe before her, but Earhart planned to follow the longest possible route by flying close to the equator. The first attempt failed when her plane broke down in Hawaii. For her second try, she took off from Miami with her navigator, Frank Noonan, heading out over the Atlantic.

Sadly, this was her last flight. After four weeks, Earhart and Noonan had completed about three quarters of the planned route, which was about twenty-two thousand miles. On July 2, 1937, they neared Howland Island in the central Pacific, but their twin-engine plane never reached the island. It simply disappeared. The US Navy and Coast Guard searched frantically for Earhart and Noonan, but no trace of them or their aircraft was found. America mourned the loss of this pioneer of the sky, whose courage had lifted the spirits of her fellow Americans. Earhart's disappearance remains one of America's greatest mysteries.

Amelia Earhart's disappearance is one of history's great mysteries.

Farm cooperatives did not help America's suffering farmers.

Farm Cooperatives

While urban Americans in the early 1930s were suddenly forced to deal with a collapsing economy, America's farmers had been suffering financial decline since 1922. Huge surpluses had driven down the prices of agricultural products. Throughout the 1920s, agricultural exports, crop prices, and land values were in a constant decline. During those years, farm families—then about 25 percent of America's population—struggled to maintain their rural lifestyle. They continued to hope that things would someday get better. But when the 1930s arrived, things got much worse.

President Hoover realized that farmers were in trouble. One of his first acts as president was to call Congress into session in April 1929 to create a program to help farmers. The Agricultural Marketing Act set up a Federal Farm Board to help farm cooperatives (business organizations owned by workers) at local, state, and regional levels. The board bought and stored crops from the farmers. Hoover believed that farmers could best help themselves with cooperatives. Unfortunately, the program did not work. The farmers' situation continued to get worse.

Devastation of the Dust Bowl

The Great Plains had always experienced periods of drought. However, the drought that began in the early 1930s and continued through most of the decade was remarkable because of its severity. A combination of factors would create the Dust Bowl—the worst environmental disaster in United States history. As the farmlands dried out, raising crops became very difficult. Adding to the problem was the fact that many farmers had overcultivated their lands. Grass had disappeared in many places, as it was plowed under by farmers or eaten by cattle. When gusty winds began to blow over the Great Plains, the top layer of dried-out soil, no longer held down by grass, blew away. This airborne soil formed thick clouds of dust. Walls of dust, sometimes rising as high as five miles into the air, swept across the farmlands and cities of the Midwest, which turned day into night and often buried farm animals, cars, and even houses.

Thousands of farmers had been forced off the land due to financial problems even before the dust came. When Dust Bowl conditions developed, hundreds of thousands more farm families were forced to abandon their farms. The roads leading west became clogged with the worn-out vehicles of migrating farm families.

Those without vehicles had to walk. Because many of them came from Oklahoma, they came to be called Okies. Writer John Steinbeck vividly portrayed their desperation in his 1939 novel *The Grapes of Wrath*. Many of the Okies who reached California found work as migrant farmers. They were often exploited by the wealthy landowners. Living conditions were awful, work was hard, and pay was low. A migrant worker was paid ten cents for each fifty-pound box of figs he or she picked, and most could pick no more than three boxes a day. About thirty dollars was the most a worker could earn per season.

Many farmers in other parts of the country did not have to abandon their farms. They continued to produce extra crops, but this kept prices—and income—low. Finally, some help arrived. When Franklin D. Roosevelt became president in 1933, he created the Agricultural Adjustment Administration (AAA). The AAA paid farmers to reduce the size of their crops, thereby driving up the prices of agricultural goods. Ironically, because Dust Bowl conditions contributed to the reduction in crops, it also had the beneficial effect of driving up prices of farm products. By 1936, American farmers' income had increased by about 50 percent.

Another federal government program, the Soil Conservation Service (SCS), was established in 1935 to teach farmers how to protect

A large cloud of dust blows across a highway in Colorado in 1936.

WANTED

Bank robber "Baby Face" Nelson was public enemy number one.

LESTER M. GILLIS,

aliases GEORGE NELSON, "BABY FACE" NELSON, ALEX GILLIS, LESTER GILES,
"BIG GEORGE" NELSON, "JIMMIE", "JIMMY" WILLIAMS.

On June 23, 1934, HOMER S. CUMMINGS, Attorney General of the United States, under the authority vested in him by an Act of Congress approved June 6, 1934, offered a reward of

$5,000.00

for the capture of Lester M. Gillis or a reward of

$2,500.00

for information leading to the arrest of Lester M. Gillis.

DESCRIPTION

Age, 25 years; Height, 5 feet 4-3/4 inches; Weight,
133 pounds; Build, medium; Eyes, yellow and grey
slate; Hair, light chestnut; Complexion, light; Occupation, oiler.

All claims to any of the aforesaid rewards and all questions and disputes that may arise
as among claimants to the foregoing rewards shall be passed upon by the Attorney General and
his decisions shall be final and conclusive. The right is reserved to divide and allocate
portions of any of said rewards as between several claimants. No part of the aforesaid rewards shall be paid to any official or employee of the Department of Justice.

If you are in possession of any information concerning the whereabouts of Lester M. Gillis,
communicate immediately by telephone or telegraph collect to the nearest office of the Division of Investigation, United States Department of Justice, the local offices of which are set
forth on the reverse side of this notice.

The apprehension of Lester M. Gillis is sought in connection with the murder of Special
Agent W. C. Baum of the Division of Investigation near Rhinelander, Wisconsin on April 23,
1934.

JOHN EDGAR HOOVER, DIRECTOR,
DIVISION OF INVESTIGATION,
UNITED STATES DEPARTMENT OF JUSTICE,
WASHINGTON, D. C.

June 25, 1934

the soil and slow the erosion process. The SCS, through a program called the Shelterbelt Project, planted trees in various parts of the Great Plains to serve as windbreaks, thereby helping to prevent Dust Bowl conditions from developing in the future.

Criminals Rise in Popularity

The Eighteenth Amendment, banning the manufacture and sale of alcoholic beverages, had been added to the Constitution in 1919. As a result, organized crime in America had grown powerful. Bootlegging, or the sale of illegal alcohol, had become a big business. Throughout the 1920s and early 1930s, the mob, led by gangsters such as Al Capone, had provided alcohol to those Americans willing to defy the Prohibition by going to illegal bars, or speakeasies. When the government ended the Prohibition in 1933 by repealing the Eighteenth Amendment, the mob had to find other ways to get rich.

As the Depression descended on the country in the early 1930s, other criminals captured the attention of the public. For a while, some Americans viewed bank robbers as romantic outlaws striking back at a system that had failed them. As a crime wave swept the nation, newspapers were filled with stories of criminals, such as "Pretty Boy" Floyd, "Baby Face" Nelson, and John Dillinger.

During the early 1930s, Hollywood producers churned out gangster movies, such as *The Public Enemy* (1931) starring James Cagney. But as the crime wave continued, the public's tolerance began to fade. Too many innocent victims had been killed during holdups and bank robberies. One by one, the famous bank robbers were either caught or killed by the police.

The Legend of Bonnie and Clyde

Two criminals that mesmerized Americans in the early 1930s were known simply as Bonnie and Clyde. Bonnie Parker and Clyde Barrow

The End of Prohibition

America's thirteen-year ban on alcohol had failed. Originally intended to reduce crime, Prohibition instead helped gangsters grow rich selling alcohol illegally. President Roosevelt wanted to make liquor legal again, and most of the public supported him. Prohibition began in 1920 with the goal of making America more wholesome and productive. But drinkers did not simply forget about alcohol but instead found illegal ways of obtaining it. Smugglers brought liquor from other countries. It was served in secret nightclubs. A restriction on alcohol only made it more tempting.

The Twenty-First Amendment to the Constitution was ratified in 1933. It said that alcohol was no longer illegal. People celebrated the repeal of the Eighteenth Amendment (*above*). Gangsters could no longer profit from the sale of alcohol. The government began taxing legal liquor sales, and these taxes helped the government fight the Great Depression.

robbed gas stations, stores, and banks. Texans in their early twenties, they led a gang that included Clyde's brother, Marvin Barrow, and Marvin's wife, Blanche. From 1932 to 1934, the Barrow Gang ran wild through the south-central United States.

Clyde Barrow had been in trouble with the law since his teens. Before joining him, Bonnie Parker was a waitress who enjoyed writing poetry and smoking cigars. The Barrow Gang usually eluded police. Sometimes they escaped only after a fierce gun battle.

Americans read about the gang's adventures in newspapers. Some people began cheering for Bonnie and Clyde. The gang always released its hostages unharmed after an escape and often gave the freed hostages money to get home. To many people, it all seemed like harmless fun. In reality, Bonnie and Clyde were suspected of committing more than a dozen murders.

Public opinion turned against Bonnie and Clyde in April 1934. The gang killed two Texas policemen in cold blood. A month later, Bonnie and Clyde were caught in a police ambush near Arcadia, Louisiana. They died in a hail of bullets. Today, the legend of Bonnie and Clyde continues to fascinate people. The story of the young outlaws has been told in numerous books and films.

The Kidnapping of the Century

Pilot Charles Lindbergh had become a national hero in 1927 for being the first person to fly solo across the Atlantic Ocean. People all over the world celebrated the feat.

Lindbergh remained famous for years. For privacy, he and his wife moved to a quiet estate in New Jersey to raise a family. On March 1, 1932, their small son, Charles Jr., was kidnapped. The Lindberghs found a ransom note in his nursery and a wooden ladder beneath the window. The kidnapping made newspaper headlines for months.

Jigsaw Puzzles

In their spare time, Americans spent countless hours bent over tables trying to fit together the pieces of jigsaw puzzles. The first puzzles in the early 1930s were made of plywood, and they were expensive. But by 1934, inexpensive jigsaw puzzles were being made out of heavy cardboard.

Within a few months, 3.5 million jigsaw puzzles had been distributed. Those who could not afford to buy jigsaw puzzles could rent them. The jigsaw puzzle craze swept the nation and continued throughout the rest of the decade. As one avid puzzle fan put it, "I like puzzles because when I put them together I don't have to think."

Charles Lindbergh made two ransom payments for the baby, but he never saw his young son alive again. In May 1932, the baby's body was found in a wooded area near the Lindbergh home. In 1934, a German immigrant named Bruno Hauptmann was arrested for the crime. Hauptmann insisted he was innocent, but at his trial the following year, a jury found him guilty. He was executed in 1936.

As a result of the Lindbergh case, Congress changed the nation's kidnapping laws. The new laws gave the FBI more power to investigate kidnappings.

The Depression's Impact on Fashion

A new look in women's fashion emerged in the 1930s in America. In response to the economic crisis, designers created clothing that was more affordable and featured a quality of timeless elegance in contrast to the flamboyant flapper look of the 1920s. Hemlines were longer, and slim waistlines were emphasized. Typical, practical, everyday women's wear consisted of a simple print dress belted just above the hips and falling five inches below the knee. Women's shoes had lower heels. Women tended to use less makeup and prefer a more natural look. Toward the end of the decade, broader shoulders became popular in both women's and men's clothing. The wide padded shoulders contrasted dramatically with narrow waistlines.

Because of hard times, women now wore the same dresses from one season to the next instead of buying new outfits. Accessories such as hats, pocketbooks, shoes, gloves, and jewelry—especially costume jewelry—became more important. The accessories created the impression of a new look while the woman wore the same dress or suit on different occasions.

While most Americans coped as best they could during the Great Depression and saved money when it came to clothing, America's wealthy threw lavish parties and debutante balls. The women of high society continued to buy fancy outfits from top designers in Paris. But the fact that most American women could no longer afford expensive clothing created an opportunity for American designers, such as Elizabeth Hawes, to produce affordable yet stylish outfits. In 1932, a woman could buy a checkered dress and dark coat combination designed by Hawes for $10.75, which was one-tenth the cost of her custom pieces. Meanwhile, in Hollywood, costume designer Adrian was creating elegant clothes for stars such as Marlene Dietrich, Joan Crawford, and Greta Garbo. Adrian's styles would influence other American designers, who were responding to the American woman's interest in the fashion styles of the stars.

Desperate to Win Money

Many Americans had had their hopes and dreams wrecked by the Depression. Others were forced to live with lowered expectations for achieving financial security. It is no wonder that so many were captivated by a board game called Monopoly, which first became available in 1935. Players could, for a moment, become rich beyond their wildest dreams—at least in their imaginations. Another game, Bingo, also appeared in 1935. Although some criticized it as a legal form of gambling, it became popular all over the country. At least in this game, one could win real money.

Perhaps the most popular get-rich-quick scheme was the chain letter. In the spring of 1935, the first chain letters began arriving. The source of the letters is unknown. But before long, millions of Americans around the country were caught up in the frenzy of a new national craze. Those who received a letter frantically scratched out the name at the top of the list of six names, added their own name at the bottom, and mailed the letter, along with a dime, to the person whose name had been at the top of the list. Chain-letter participants expected to receive a payment of 15,625

Hollywood star Greta Garbo wore Adrian's elegant creations.

The popular board game Monopoly was introduced in 1935.

dimes once the letter had been passed along by five more people, but the scheme did not work. Still, post offices around the nation were so overwhelmed by the millions of chain letters that they had to hire extra help. Eventually, the excitement faded when people failed to receive their $1,562.50 in the mail.

Entertainment and the Arts

After being elected in 1932, President Roosevelt went to work to try to end the Great Depression. The programs he started were called the New Deal. While trying to help the ordinary American citizen, the Roosevelt administration also increased government regulation of banking and business. Safety measures, such as Social Security, were put into place.

Works Progress Administration

As part of his New Deal, President Roosevelt set up a work-relief agency known as the Works Progress Administration (WPA). The WPA paid for about 125,000 public buildings, such as post offices, to be built and created more than 8 million jobs in the process. The Federal Art Project (FAP), a part of the WPA, paid for art projects—murals, paintings, and sculptures—often to decorate the new public buildings built by the WPA. By 1939, FAP-funded muralists, painters, and sculptors had completed 1,300 murals, 48,100 paintings, and more than 3,500 sculptures.

Part of Roosevelt's New Deal was the Works Progress Administration.

King Kong *entertained audiences during the Depression.*

The huge new murals often depicted the struggles of the working class in a style known as social realism. Many of the artists were influenced by the great Mexican muralist Diego Rivera. Among the artists employed by the FAP were Thomas Hart Benton, Grant Wood, and Jackson Pollock. Other WPA art programs included the Federal Theatre Project, the Federal Writers Project, and the Federal Music Project. All of these New Deal programs put artists to work producing government-sponsored books, music, and shows.

Hollywood's Golden Age

What could be a more pleasant way to spend an afternoon than attending a matinee at the local movie theater? For the unemployed, movies provided a perfect escape from boredom and despair—at least for a couple of hours. This escape was possible, of course, if one had the twenty-five-cent price of admission.

Millions of Americans flocked to the movies during the Depression, and Hollywood provided a wide choice of fantasies, such as *Dracula* (1931) starring Bela Lugosi, *Frankenstein* (1931) starring Boris Karloff, and *King Kong* (1933). There were also lavish musicals, such as *42nd Street* (1933) with elaborate dance numbers directed by Busby Berkeley, and *Flying Down to Rio* (1933) with Fred Astaire and Ginger Rogers. Gangster movies such as *Little Caesar* (1930) starring Edward G. Robinson were popular, as were comedies such as *Duck Soup* (1933) starring the Marx brothers. People enjoyed Westerns such as *Stagecoach* (1939) starring John Wayne, mystery films such as *The Thin Man* (1934) starring William Powell and Myrna Loy, and adventure films such as *Mutiny on the Bounty* (1935) starring Charles Laughton.

In 1935, *Becky Sharp*, the first feature-length movie filmed in a color process called Technicolor, was released. Although the color was far from perfect, audiences who were used to films in black and

Shirley Temple

When Americans in the 1930s saw Shirley Temple in her first starring role in *Stand Up and Cheer* (1934), they went wild over the five-year-old Hollywood star. Perhaps her innocent smiling face, dimples, and curly hair evoked memories of happier times, which audiences of the 1930s must have yearned for. Americans could not get enough of the little actress.

Soon, her face was appearing on books, ribbons, and buttons. Americans bought millions of Shirley Temple dolls and coloring books, and Shirley Temple look-alike contests were held throughout the country. A nonalcoholic cocktail, made from ginger ale and a dash of grenadine and served with a maraschino cherry, was even named after her, and it became popular with young people.

white were amazed by the new element of realism. In 1938, Walt Disney released the animated film *Snow White and the Seven Dwarfs*, his first feature-length cartoon. The following year, two of the most popular movies of all time were released: the musical fantasy *The Wizard of Oz,* starring Judy Garland, and the Civil War epic *Gone With the Wind*, starring Clark Gable and Vivien Leigh. *Gone with the Wind* sold more tickets than any other film in Hollywood history. The record still stands today.

The Popularity of Radio

When they were not watching movies, Americans turned to another immensely popular entertainment—the radio. The 1930s were truly the golden age of radio. Radio listeners could find just about any type of entertainment they wanted. There were all kinds of romance, mystery, and adventure shows. The art of sound effects was perfected so that audiences listening to a couple of coconut shells on a soundboard believed they heard the hooves of the Lone Ranger's horse, Silver. The airwaves were also filled with all kinds of music, including live broadcasts from the Metropolitan Opera in New York and the NBC Symphony Orchestra, conducted by Arturo Toscanini, as well as popular swing bands and jazz singers. Comedians such as George Burns, Gracie Allen, Jack Benny, and Ed Wynn became radio stars. Sports broadcasts were also popular, as were quiz shows and amateur hours.

War of the Worlds

By the mid-1930s, radio stations began broadcasting the news. Millions of Americans got into the habit of relying on their local radio stations, in addition to newspapers, for information. Perhaps that is why the reaction of hundreds of thousands of Americans to Orson Welles's radio broadcast of H. G. Wells's 1898 novel *The War of the Worlds* should not have been so surprising.

On Sunday evening, October 30, 1938, Orson Welles, on the radio program *Mercury Theater on the Air*, began describing a frightful event—the landing of Martian invaders in New Jersey! Most listeners had missed the introductory comments stating that the broadcast was an adaptation of a work of fiction. They believed that the shocking report they were hearing was an actual news report. Widespread panic occurred in various parts of the country as Welles related details about the Martians' weapons and their power. Because the broadcast terrified so many Americans, CBS radio had to agree to never again broadcast a make-believe news event.

Swinging with the Big Bands

Jazz clarinet player Benny Goodman watched in amazement from the bandstand as energetic couples on the dance floor threw themselves with wild abandon into the intricate steps of the jitterbug, the new dance craze that was sweeping the nation. Goodman marveled at the athletic steps of the dance partners, who at times seemed more like acrobats than dancers. Goodman later said, "Their eyes popped, their heads pecked, their feet tapped out the time, arms jerked to the rhythm."

In the mid-1930s, Goodman, who came to be called the King of Swing, and other bandleaders, such as Tommy Dorsey, Glenn Miller, Count Basie, and Duke Ellington, played a style of jazz known as swing. Live radio broadcasts helped make the music popular. Featuring sophisticated big-band arrangements, swing was not only good to listen to, but its faster beat also made it great to dance to. For the next ten years, swing would be the most popular kind of music in America. Jazz singers who appeared with the bands, such as Ella Fitzgerald, Helen O'Connell, and Billie Holiday, also became popular.

Swing music inspired a number of fast-paced dance steps. The Lindy Hop was named after pilot Charles Lindbergh. Chicago, New

From Pulp Fiction to Comic Books

During the Great Depression, many people could not afford books. For a dime or less, readers could escape into a world of adventure and superheroes. Low-cost magazines were printed on cheap, grainy paper called pulp. They had titles such as *Amazing Stories*, *Dime Detective*, and *Flying Aces*. Pulp magazines contained short stories of action and adventure. Often these stories were poorly written. Publishers relied on colorful and exciting cover art to sell their magazines. Artists created dazzling images of horror, mystery, science fiction, and romance. Authors then wrote stories that matched the cover art. Despite their low quality, pulp magazines were fun and amusing.

Comic books also became standard reading in the 1930s. They began as reprints of newspaper cartoons. Readers were won over. Soon, brand new comics appeared on newsstands. Comic book sales soared in 1938. That year, Superman made his debut in *Action Comics*. A year later, Batman made his first appearance in *Detective Comics*. The superheroes quickly gained legions of young readers.

York, and Kansas City were swing hot spots. Radio stations carried live big-band performances from these cities.

"Strange Fruit"

When African-American singer Billie Holiday went on the road as a jazz vocalist with Artie Shaw's all-white band, she was often the target of racism, especially in the South. Intolerance and hatred against minorities remained an ugly reality in many places. During the 1930s in the South, acts of racist brutality were still occurring. There were incidents of African Americans being lynched (killed as punishment for an alleged crime without a trial) each year. In one famous case in Scottsboro, Alabama, in 1931, nine young African American men who were falsely accused of raping two white women were nearly lynched by a mob. But the officials prevented this and the nine stood trial. All were convicted of the crime. Eight were sentenced to death, and the other—a twelve-year-old—was given a life sentence. Ultimately, after years of legal battles, the convictions were over-turned. But other African Americans in similar situations were not so "lucky."

In 1939, twenty-four-year-old Billie Holiday recorded a song called "Strange Fruit." It was her personal protest against racism and lynch-ing. The lyrics, written by poet Lewis Allen, began:

Southern trees bear a strange fruit
Blood on the leaves and blood at the root
Black body swinging in the Southern breeze
Strange fruit hanging from the poplar trees

Jazz singer Billie Holiday was known as Lady Day.

Mildred "Babe" Didrikson impressed at the 1932 Olympics.

Sports

Athletics are good exercise and entertainment. However, in the 1930s sports took on more importance. Some events grew beyond a contest between athletes. They became part of a rivalry between nations and races.

One Babe's Exit Makes Room for Another

Sports were one of America's most popular diversions during the Great Depression, and the favorite sport continued to be America's pastime—baseball. In 1932, New York Yankees baseball star George Herman "Babe" Ruth's fabulous career was winding down as he played in his last World Series against the Chicago Cubs. Americans would miss Babe Ruth's home runs.

But there was another "Babe" in American sports, a woman whose career was about to take off in 1932. She could play baseball, basketball, football, tennis, and golf. She also excelled at swimming and track and field. She even boxed. When it came to sports, there was not much that Mildred "Babe" Didrikson could not do. Because she was such an amazing all-around athlete, it seemed a pretty safe bet that she would put on an impressive performance in the 1932 summer Olympics in Los Angeles. Earlier that year, Didrikson entered eight of

Major League Baseball's First Night Game

On May 24, 1935, professional baseball changed forever when President Franklin Delano Roosevelt switched on the lights at Crosley Field in Cincinatti. This marked major league baseball's first ever night game.

Until this night, baseball games were played during the day. However, night games became so popular that they soon became the norm and the term day game was used to distinguish afternoon games.

This wasn't the first time lights had been used in professional baseball, however. The Negro Leagues were known for illuminating fields with headlights from gathered cars and trucks. And minor league teams had been hosting night games for around five years in order to make as much money as possible once the Depression hit.

ten events in the National Women's Track and Field Championships. There, she won five events and tied one. At the Olympics, she won a gold medal in the javelin throw and in the eighty-meter hurdles and set world records in both events. Americans were proud of their new Olympic star.

The 1936 Summer Olympics

During the Depression, some hopeless people who felt they had nothing to lose considered replacing the American system of government. Other models were available, including fascism in Germany. In some places in Europe, people eager for change threw their support behind power-hungry dictators, believed their promises, and accepted their lies.

The 1936 summer Olympics were held in Berlin. Germany's dictator, Adolf Hitler, hoped to use the Olympics to win a major propaganda victory for his Nazi beliefs. Hitler's wish was for Germany's athletes to walk away with all the gold medals and prove to the world the superiority of their so-called Aryan race. Hitler asked his personal filmmaker, Leni Riefenstahl, to document the Nazi victories at the games.

Athletes from many countries had mixed feelings about going to Berlin. Hitler had already begun his persecution of Jews in Germany and had made known his racist views regarding other peoples. But the athletes had spent years of hard work training for the Olympics, and they chose to participate.

Before the US Olympic Committee agreed to American participation in the games, it received Hitler's guarantee that there would be no discrimination against African American or Jewish American athletes. Ultimately, 328 athletes from the United States went to Berlin. Among them were ten African Americans and many Jews.

Hitler's plan to score a propaganda victory backfired. Jesse Owens, an African American athlete, won four gold medals in the sprint and long jump events and was named Athlete of the Games. Owens proved to be the most popular figure of the 1936 Olympics. The ten African American athletes walked away with a total of eight gold, three silver, and two bronze medals. Hitler did not bother to stick around and congratulate Jesse Owens and his teammates.

Joe Louis

Because boxing was illegal in many areas of the United States at the turn of the twentieth century, it had fewer fans than most other sports. In 1920, however, New York legalized boxing and was soon followed by other states. By the 1930s, boxing had not only become a popular spectator sport, but it was also in a golden age of popularity.

Germans and African Americans also clashed in professional boxing. A huge match took place in New York in 1936 when German heavyweight Max Schmeling fought African American boxer Joe Louis. The powerful Louis suffered his first loss, and Max Schmeling returned to Germany a hero. However, Louis became the heavyweight champion when he defeated James J. Braddock in June 1937. And in a 1938 rematch with Max Schmelling, Louis easily defeated the German in just one round.

Louis was perhaps the most famous boxer of the 1930s. He defended his heavyweight title twenty-five times, holding the title longer than any other boxer, from 1937 until he retired in 1949.

Match of the Century

Horse racing was hugely popular in the 1930s. One race in 1938 was dubbed the match of the century. Unlike a regular horse race, which usually includes six to twelve horses, a match race includes only two contenders. It pitted a small spirited horse named Seabiscuit against the powerful champion War Admiral. On November 1, a crowd of about forty thousand people came to see the race at Pimlico Race Course in Maryland. Forty million more listened to Seabiscuit's victory over the radio. Many Americans were rooting for the underdog Seabiscuit. They cheered him on to a stunning upset victory.

National and International Politics

In 1924, Congress had passed a bill promising the veterans a cash bonus in appreciation for their service to their country. According to the law, however, they would not receive it until 1945.

Bonus Army Marches on Washington

By the spring of 1932, veterans were tired of waiting for their money. The Great Depression was hard on them, like everyone else. The former soldiers needed money to feed their families. They demanded that their bonuses be paid early. More than seventeen thousand angry veterans from all over the United States traveled to Washington, D.C., to protest. Newspapers called them the Bonus Army.

In mid-June, the US Senate rejected a bill to pay the bonuses early. Discouraged, some of the veterans who had gone to Washington gave up and went home. But thousands vowed to stay until their demands were met. Some occupied old government buildings not far from the Capitol and the White House. Others lived in camps. The largest of these camps was located across the Anacostia River in an area known as Anacostia Flats.

War veterans gathered to demand the bonus they had been promised.

US Army troops used violence to break up the Bonus Army's camp.

On July 28, a group of protesters clashed with local police along Pennsylvania Avenue. President Hoover ordered the surrounding area to be cleared of demonstrators. US Army troops under the command of General Douglas MacArthur moved in. MacArthur would become a hero during World War II, but on this day, his conduct was questionable. After forcibly clearing the area around Pennsylvania Avenue, he ignored orders to halt. Instead, MacArthur had his soldiers pursue the retreating veterans across the Anacostia River. A riot broke out. MacArthur's troops destroyed the Bonus Army's camp. They beat Bonus Army veterans. Dozens of the veterans were injured, and at least two died. In the process, the troops accidentally killed an eleven-month-old baby with tear gas. The incident shocked many Americans, who felt that the violence was unnecessary. Four years later, Congress gave the veterans their early bonus payments.

Tariff Backfires

At first, President Herbert Hoover hoped the economy would eventually fix itself. He considered the Depression a natural cycle in business. When events proved him wrong, Hoover took action. He signed the Hawley-Smoot Tariff Act into law on June 17, 1930 in hopes that raising tariffs on imported goods would increase the market share for American products. A tariff is a fee paid on goods imported or exported that is often used to encourage consumers to buy domestic products.

Unfortunately, Hawley-Smoot caused America's trading partners to raise tariffs on American goods, as well, which caused a decline in American exports. In turn, production had to decrease and more jobs were lost. Hawley-Smoot was also a final blow to many American farmers who could no longer export their produce. Hoover would try other policies to fix the problems being caused by the Great Depression, but it would take another President to succeed.

Roosevelt's New Deal

Americans were tired of Hoover's Republican administration, and they voted for change—for the Democratic candidate, Franklin Delano Roosevelt. At his inauguration on March 4, 1933, Roosevelt told the American people, "The only thing we have to fear is fear itself. … This nation asks for action, and action now. We must act and act quickly." President Roosevelt made it clear to his cabinet that they had to experiment with new ideas to solve the problems of the Depression. If one approach did not work, they must try something else.

Roosevelt's actions would forever change the role of American government. Roosevelt's collection of federal government programs, known as the New Deal, was aimed at reviving the economy and putting Americans back to work. In responding to the needs of the ordinary American, New Deal legislation increased the power and size of the federal government. Ironically, many New Deal programs were modeled on policies Hoover and his so-called do-nothing administration had tried first. Roosevelt advisor Rexford Tugwell later said, "We didn't admit it at the time [1933], but practically the whole New Deal was extrapolated [taken] from programs that Hoover started."

One of Roosevelt's first acts in office was to declare a nationwide weeklong bank holiday. During this time, withdrawals were banned, the US Treasury Department examined the banks' books, and Congress passed the Emergency Banking Relief Act. The president now had the power to regulate banking transactions. Nine thousand banks had failed by 1933 and nine million savings accounts had been wiped out. Customers panicked by rumors of bank problems withdrew all their money, which forced banks that lacked the money to pay what they owed to all their customers to close. To reassure the public and

Young men head to their new reforestation jobs created by the New Deal.

The CCC preserved and developed America's natural resources.

gain support for his actions, Roosevelt gave a fireside chat on the radio. Later in 1933, the government created the Federal Deposit Insurance Corporation (FDIC) to insure deposits of up to $5,000 in all national and state banks in the Federal Reserve System.

Among the many important New Deal programs was the Civilian Conservation Corps (CCC). It provided jobs for about two million young men. The jobs involved the preservation of the environment through such measures as planting trees. The AAA helped farmers. The WPA made construction jobs available, as well as work for artists. The Federal Emergency Relief Administration (FERA) funded state programs. The Tennessee Valley Authority (TVA) was set up to build dams and produce electricity in the impoverished Tennessee Valley.

The National Recovery Administration (NRA) administered one of the most controversial programs, the National Industrial Recovery Act (NIRA), which had the power to regulate competition and labor practices, set minimum wages, and stabilize prices. Of course, many businesses opposed the NRA. And in 1935, the US Supreme Court declared the Roosevelt administration and Congress had exceeded their authority and that the NRA was unconstitutional. However, Roosevelt was reelected in 1936, and he managed to reinstate some of the NRA's main ideas in later New Deal laws.

Unionizing America

The words of Florence Reece's famous union song "Which Side Are You On?" called upon America's workers to choose sides in the ongoing battle between labor and management. And choose sides they did. In the 1930s, working people developed a sense of solidarity like never before. There was a shared sense of anger and resentment at the capitalist system that had brought on the Great Depression. Union membership soared as workers sought to protect their jobs and participate in strikes for better working conditions. Others who identified the wealthy and powerful as their class enemies were inspired by the social progress and fairer distribution of wealth they believed was occurring in the communist Soviet Union. Known as progressives, they joined leftist political organizations, such as the communist party or the socialist party. Communists believe that the government should own all property while distributing money and other goods to people according to their needs. Socialists are less radical, believing that the government should take steps to regulate the way businesses are run in order to protect the working people. It seemed to many that the only way to improve life in America would be to replace the capitalist system with a different one.

President Roosevelt was determined to make the existing capitalist system work to fill the needs of America's workers. He introduced legislation in support of unionization, and in 1935, Congress passed the National Labor Relations Act (NLRA). Now labor was guaranteed the right to unionize, and companies were forbidden to try to break up unions. The labor movement grew stronger when labor leader John L. Lewis, President of the United Mine Workers of America (UMWA), left the American Federation of Labor (AFL) to form the Congress of Industrial Organizations (CIO) because the AFL would not admit unskilled workers. In 1936 and 1937, the CIO organized a wave of successful sit-down strikes involving about half a million workers in the automobile and steel industries. Folk singers, such as Woody Guthrie, traveled around the country and sang songs about the unions and the struggles of working people. By the end of the decade, nearly all of America's major industries were unionized.

African-American Unemployment Soars

If life during the Great Depression was difficult for many white Americans, it was even worse for African Americans. While prejudice

Workers gathered to demand the right to unionize.

African Americans struggled with high unemployment rates.

was nothing new to African Americans, job discrimination during the 1930s was especially severe in the North, as well as in the South. When employers needed to reduce the number of their employees, African Americans were usually the first to be fired. And because of racial prejudice, many employers, given the choice, preferred to hire an inexperienced white over an experienced African American whenever they had a position to fill.

Unemployed whites took jobs that they would have avoided in the past, having considered them too menial, such as garbage collector, street sweeper, or elevator operator. In so doing, they took away the only jobs that many African Americans had ever done. Also, many families could no longer afford to hire servants, which put many African American women out of work.

In 1932, the unemployment rate for African Americans stood at an average of 48 percent compared to 25 percent for whites. In some places, the unemployment rate for African Americans was much higher. For example, it was 70 percent in the city of Pittsburgh, Pennsylvania. By 1932, churches and private charities that had been providing a bare minimum level of relief to African American families had used up their resources.

Fortunately, the early New Deal programs helped African Americans by providing food, shelter, clothing, and jobs. The CCC hired black youths to work in integrated conservation camps. The National Youth Administration (NYA) provided student relief programs that allowed young African American men and women to stay in school. The WPA's Federal Art Project provided jobs for African American artists and taught almost a quarter of a million blacks to read and write. And the Public Works Administration (PWA) reserved more than one third of the housing units it built for African Americans.

The Roosevelt administration also acted in other ways to help African Americans. President Roosevelt sought the advice of civil rights activists, such as Walter White, the head of the National Association for the Advancement of Colored People (NAACP); union leader A. Philip Randolph; Mary McLeod Bethune; and others. Roosevelt's unofficial black cabinet would become the Federal Council on Negro Affairs, headed by Mary Bethune.

First Lady Eleanor Roosevelt gave speeches, made radio broadcasts, and wrote newspaper editorials for the cause of racial equality. She helped secure positions for African Americans in the Roosevelt administration, which tripled the number of blacks working for the federal government. And in 1939, she resigned from the Daughters of the American Revolution (DAR) because the organization had refused to allow African American opera singer Marian Anderson to perform at Washington's Constitution Hall, which was owned by the DAR.

Mexican Americans Sent Back to Mexico

The Great Depression caused hardship and suffering for many minority groups, especially for Mexican Americans. Thousands of Mexican Americans lost their jobs and joined the growing ranks of unemployed Americans. The Roosevelt administration tried to help them. The Federal Emergency Relief Administration provided temporary work to Mexican American workers, and some Mexican American carpenters, masons, and unskilled laborers were hired by the WPA to build bridges, libraries, and other structures. But unemployed whites did not want to compete with Mexican Americans or illegal Mexican immigrants for job openings.

A growing repatriation movement to force Mexicans and Mexican Americans to return to Mexico gained wide support. The US Department of Labor began a program of voluntary repatriation or forced deportation. More than four hundred thousand Mexican American and Mexican *repatriados* were sent back to Mexico during the 1930s. Among them were many first-generation Mexican Americans and

Walter White led the NAACP for a quarter of a century.

John Collier promoted the rights of American Indians.

many whose families had lived in America for many generations. Naturally, they felt rejected and betrayed by their country—the United States.

John Collier and Indian Reorganization

During the 1930s, Roosevelt's New Deal included a radical new deal for American Indians, too. Government policy toward Indians had long been one of Americanization, or forced assimilation and the eradication of traditional tribal customs and beliefs. Under the Roosevelt administration, John Collier, a strong supporter of Indian rights, became Commissioner of Indian Affairs. Under his leadership, the Bureau of Indian Affairs hired more Indians and gave them greater authority than ever before. Collier promoted tribal social and religious ceremonies, such as the Sun Dance and the use of tribal languages. Indian medical practices were accepted, and arts and crafts were encouraged.

In 1933, the New Deal's Civilian Conservation Corps (CCC) included an Indian division that provided jobs for young Indian men. The Indian Reorganization Act of 1934 incorporated Collier's policies of ending forced assimilation and supporting cultural pluralism. It also ended the policy of allotment of reservation lands dating back to 1887. The policy of allotment involved breaking up the reservation and allotting a small private parcel of land to each Indian family. The Indian Reorganization Act provided funds to tribes for the repurchase of lands lost because of the allotment policy. Between 1934 and 1937, Indian tribes added more than two million acres to their existing lands.

America Tries to Stay Neutral

During the 1930s, the world was becoming an increasingly dangerous place. Fascist dictators were drawing up plans for territorial conquest, and before long, their armies would be on the march. Wars would break out in various places overseas and would eventually threaten to engulf more and more nations. But the majority of Americans during the 1930s, preoccupied with trying to survive the Depression, had no desire to get involved in problems overseas. Isolationist sentiments were so strong in America that the United States had never even become a member of the League of Nations, formed after World War I, the purpose of which was to keep peace in the world.

Secure in the knowledge that two very wide oceans separated the United States from Europe and Asia, most Americans were isolationists. They wanted to sit back and look the other way as the rest of the world fell apart. This would be impossible, however, because of America's economic interests abroad.

Japan Launches All-Out War Against China

To America's west on the other side of the Pacific Ocean, Japan had invaded and occupied Manchuria in northern China in 1931 and set up a puppet government. The Japanese military had taken control of Japan's civilian government and blamed it for the Depression that was affecting not only the United States but the entire world. The military kept Emperor Hirohito as head of state, thus winning popular support for its actions. The League of Nations condemned Japan's aggression but was powerless to stop it, and in 1933, Japan withdrew from the league. The Japanese planned to conquer the rest of China, and in 1937, Japan embarked on an all-out war of aggression against them. Japan intended to establish a Pacific empire.

The events leading to war had begun years earlier. Since the 1920s, Japan was completely under the control of its military. Japanese citizens worked solely toward building the armed forces and creating a powerful war machine. Meanwhile, the officers in charge made plans to expand the Japanese Empire. Close by and poorly defended, China

US planes drop ammunition for the Chinese to fight Japan.

Japan's invasion would devastate China for years.

was an obvious place to start. China also had large amounts of iron, coal, and open land.

The situation in China was very different. In 1911, the nation underwent a revolution. The revolution ended more than two thousand years of rule by emperors. Afterward, rival groups fought for control of the country. The two major groups were the nationalists, led by Chiang Kai-shek, and the communists, led by Mao Zedong. Their ongoing fight weakened China and put it at risk of invasion by a foreign country.

Japan's army began its conquest in 1931. For the next six years, the Japanese made small but steady gains. During this time, China's warring groups fought with each other as much as they did with the invaders.

In July 1937, heavy fighting broke out. Japanese troops moved on Beijing. The nationalists and the communists finally agreed to set aside their differences. They united against a common enemy. The early months of the war went poorly for the Chinese. The Japanese soldiers had better weapons and training.

Within six months, Japan's army reached the walled city of Nanjing, China's capital. Once inside, Japanese soldiers ravaged the city. For six weeks, they tortured and murdered its residents. The death toll from the Nanjing massacre is unknown, but modern estimates place it between 150,000 and 300,000 people.

The brutal war would drag on for years. Chinese forces continued to retreat as the Japanese soldiers followed them deeper into Chinese territory. Japan's war in China would eventually sap its military strength. It would also hamper Japan's efforts against America in World War II.

The Nazis Take Control of Germany and Establish the Axis

To America's east across the Atlantic Ocean, brutal fascist dictators were in control of Italy and Germany, and anyone paying attention to developments there would have had good reason to fear the worst. Italy's Benito Mussolini, who had come to power in 1922, was envious of the British and French colonial empires in Africa. Hoping to carve out an Italian empire in Africa, Mussolini ordered an invasion of Ethiopia in 1935. In 1936, Ethiopia's exiled Emperor Haile Selassie appealed to the League of Nations for help, warning, "It is us today. It will be you tomorrow." But the league did nothing.

Meanwhile in Germany, Adolf Hitler and his National Socialist German Workers' (Nazi) party were in power. Hitler, who had been named Chancellor (chief executive officer) of Germany in 1933, assumed total power in 1934 when President Paul Ludwig von Hindenburg died. Hitler, who believed minorities, especially Jews, were inferior to Germans, or Aryans, took control of every aspect of German life. He began to pass laws that deprived German Jews of most of their rights. Hitler's Gestapo murdered hundreds of the Nazis' political opponents. But most Germans, impressed with Hitler's success in putting Germans back to work and rebuilding Germany's devastated economy, gave him their support. Indeed, they were delighted with their new highways and the rebuilding of Germany's armed forces. And they were especially thrilled by their führer's (leader's) strong speeches at mass rallies and on the radio. They listened, spellbound, as Hitler proclaimed the birth of Germany's Third Reich (empire), which he said would last for at least a thousand years.

Soon Hitler was ready to test the resolve of the other major European powers—France and Great Britain. Unfortunately, the desire of those two nations to keep the peace in Europe would lead them to

The League of Nations

Created after World War I, the League of Nations was a group of forty-two countries working together to avoid future wars. The League of Nations struggled during the 1930s. Powerful dictators were threatening war. In the end, the League was helpless to stop them.

US President Woodrow Wilson first proposed the League of Nations, but the United States never joined. This weakened the league. There were other problems, as well. Member countries refused to compromise for the benefit of all. Even worse, the league was unable to punish hostile nations, such as Japan, Germany, and Italy. As the world drifted closer to another war, it became obvious the league would be unable to meet its original goal. The League of Nations fizzled and formally disbanded in 1946.

Despite its many flaws, the League of Nations was valuable. It was an important first step toward global cooperation. Eventually, the United Nations would replace it. The United Nations learned from the league's mistakes. Today, diplomats from 192 countries meet at the UN headquarters in New York City.

adopt a policy of appeasement, or giving in, toward Hitler that would ultimately lead to a world war. Hitler was determined to defy the Treaty of Versailles, which Germany and the Allies had signed in 1919 to end World War I.

The treaty had required Germany to accept full responsibility for the war and to pay huge war reparations, or debts paid as punishment, to the victors. These payments had wrecked the German economy in the 1920s. Hitler ignored the treaty's prohibition against rebuilding Germany's armed forces. And in March 1936, Hitler sent his troops to occupy the Rhineland, a thirty-mile-wide area of Germany bordering France, which, according to the treaty, was to remain free from military use. France and Great Britain did nothing about it. Hitler was encouraged by this. By October 1936, Germany, Italy, and Japan had become allies known as the Axis Powers.

Spain's Civil War

In July 1936 in Spain, General Francisco Franco, who had won the support of Spanish military leaders, set out to overthrow the country's democratically elected government. His goal was to do away with the republic and establish a fascist dictatorship with himself in charge. Franco's revolt would result in three years of civil war.

In January 1937, the war was at a stalemate. Neither the loyalists, who supported the democratic government, nor Franco's nationalist fascists could gain the upper hand. The US Congress had passed a Neutrality Act forbidding the sale of arms to either side. Hitler and Mussolini, however, had no such laws restraining them. By April 1937, one hundred thousand Italian soldiers were fighting in Spain for the nationalists, and Hitler sent his Condor Legion, a unit of warplanes, to help defeat the loyalists. On April 27, the Condor Legion bombed the city of Guernica, Spain, destroyed the town, and killed

Soviet Citizens Suffer

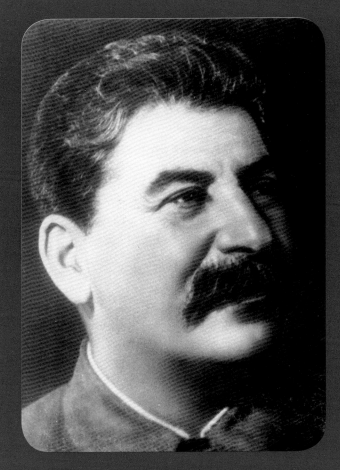

In the Soviet Union, communist dictator Joseph Stalin strengthened his iron-fisted rule by executing many high-ranking military officers and communist party officials during a five-year-long purge of those Stalin considered enemies of the state.

He also sent as many as ten million Soviet citizens to labor camps in Siberia, where many died. Also during the 1930s, Stalin forced Soviet farms to collectivize, or join together under the common ownership of the government. This change in traditional farming caused widespread famine when the central government's agricultural plans failed.

Adolf Hitler was charismatic, hungry for power, and dangerous.

sixteen hundred of its citizens. Spanish painter Pablo Picasso created a huge painting called *Guernica* in response to this outrageous act.

Not all Americans were isolationists. At least three thousand idealistic young American men believed the time had come to stand up to the fascists. They went to Spain, where they fought for the loyalist cause as members of the Abraham Lincoln Brigade. Also in Spain to report on the war were American writers Ernest Hemingway and John Dos Passos. Both were loyalist supporters. Unfortunately, the loyalists were greatly outnumbered and outgunned, and in 1939, Franco became the dictator of Spain. In 1940, Hemingway published his novel *For Whom the Bell Tolls*, which is about the Spanish Civil War.

Hitler's "Final Solution"

Hitler blamed the Jews for all of Germany's problems. Because he was such an effective speaker, he convinced millions of Germans that he was right—that the Jews did not even deserve to be treated as human beings. Hitler's Nuremberg Laws of 1935 deprived German Jews of their citizenship. Jewish books were burned. Jewish Germans could no longer marry or do business with non-Jewish Germans. Jewish professionals were fired from their jobs. Life for German Jews steadily grew worse. Those who could made plans to leave Germany.

On the night of November 9, 1938, mobs of Germans, organized by the Nazis, attacked Jews throughout Germany and Austria. Thousands of Jewish synagogues, homes, and businesses were burned. Hundreds of Jews were beaten and dozens were killed. More than thirty thousand Jews were arrested. Because of the shattered windows in Jewish buildings and the shards of glass littering the streets, the night came to be known as Kristallnacht, or Night of Broken Glass.

Before long, the Nazis began rounding up Jews in Germany, Austria, and other Nazi-occupied countries and sending them to

How Did the Nazis Take Control?

With the benefit of hindsight, it is easy to wonder how German citizens, not to mention the rest of the world, could allow a madman like Adolf Hitler to gain so much power.

Recall that Germany had lost World War I and was forced to endure several humiliating and crippling concessions. The German people suffered terribly when the Great Depression hit. Unemployment rose, and many Germans could not feed their families. They felt they needed a strong leader to pull them out of their pit of despair. Hitler preyed on this sentiment, and soon his Nazi party was taking control of the German government. The Nazis controlled the lives of all German citizens, including children. Schools taught Nazi ideals. Boys were required to join the Hitler Youth, and girls were forced to join the League of German Girls, both of which were clubs that surrounded children with Nazi culture. Adults were constantly exposed to Nazi culture, too. Hitler ensured that all newspapers, books, and radio shows praised Nazi ideals. Propaganda seeped into every facet of German life. The Nazis also held enormous stirring rallies that created a sense of unity among the German people. People became completely devoted to Adolf Hitler.

concentration camps, where they were held as prisoners and forced to do grueling labor. Hitler eventually announced his "Final Solution" to the so-called Jewish problem—all Jews were to be killed. The concentration camps became death camps. In the early 1940s, about six million Jews would be systematically murdered in the concentration camps. The worst genocidal episode in history, this would come to be called the Holocaust.

Throughout the 1930s, Hitler's persecution of the Jews was reported in the news in America and elsewhere. Most Americans were appalled—but not all. Unfortunately, anti-Semitism, or anti-Jewish sentiment, did not exist in Germany alone. In America, there were many who supported Hitler's actions. By 1939, there were more than eight hundred fascist and anti-Semitic organizations in the United States, among them the German American Bund and radio priest Father Charles Coughlin's National Union for Social Justice.

Hitler Continues His Conquest

The French wanted peace. The English wanted peace. The horrors of World War I were still fresh in many minds. So when Hitler made a demand, the British and French gave in because they hoped to preserve peace. That is why Great Britain and France accepted Hitler's *Anschluss*, or annexation, of Austria on March 12, 1938. It is also why British Prime Minister Neville Chamberlain, on September 29 and 30 in Munich, agreed to Hitler's occupation of the Sudetenland, a Czech province inhabited mostly by Germans. With each of his demands, Hitler gave the impression that he would be satisfied and would make no further demands. But each time Hitler got what he wanted, his appetite for more territory grew stronger. In fact, he ignored the promises he made in the Munich Agreement to limit his territorial seizures. Hitler had made his desire for *lebensraum* (living space) perfectly clear, so his attempt to win more territory was not too surprising.

When Chamberlain returned to England from Munich, he told the cheering crowds that were on hand to greet him, "I believe it is peace in our time." But Winston Churchill, who would lead Great Britain during the war to come, said Munich represented "a total and unmitigated defeat." It was only the beginning—Hitler would soon want more.

Within six months, Hitler's troops took over all of Czechoslovakia. Mussolini, inspired by Hitler's success, invaded and occupied Albania. Next on Hitler's list was Poland. Although England and France had said they would guarantee Poland's independence, by this time Hitler had nothing but contempt for the British and French. He assumed they would not act. This time, however, he was wrong.

On August 23, 1939, Hitler and Soviet dictator Joseph Stalin signed a nonaggression pact. Hitler and Stalin secretly agreed to divide Poland between them. The world was shocked by this sudden turn of events. At the time, Stalin had been negotiating with Great Britain and France in the hopes of stopping Hitler's aggression. Stalin's action was especially shocking to those progressive idealists in America who had great respect for the Soviet Union's communist system.

On September 1, 1939, Hitler's troops invaded Poland in a massive surprise attack. Two days later, Great Britain and France declared war on Germany. World War II had begun, and it would change the world forever.

British Prime Minister Neville Chamberlain foolishly gave in to Hitler's demands without realizing the madman would never be appeased.

Advances in Science, Technology, and Medicine

While the country was plunged into the Great Depression, advances in the sciences continued. The 1930s saw the construction of jaw-dropping skyscrapers, the discovery of a new planet, and promises for an exciting future in America.

A New Planet

Astronomers had long suspected that the solar system contained another planet beyond the eight known planets—Mercury, Venus, Earth, Mars, Jupiter, Saturn, Uranus, and Neptune. Careful mathematical calculations of the orbit of the planet Neptune led astronomers to believe that Neptune was being influenced by the gravitational pull of another planet even farther away from the sun. Among those predicting the existence of Planet X was astronomer Percival Lowell. After Lowell's death, young astronomer Clyde W. Tombaugh took up the search. Working at Lowell Observatory in Flagstaff, Arizona, Tombaugh photographed the tiny mysterious planet close to its predicted location on February 18, 1930. Planet X was given a name from mythology—Pluto, the Greek god of the underworld.

Clyde Tombaugh
photographed Planet X,
later known as Pluto.

Pluto's Demotion

The front page of the *Chicago Daily Tribune* read "See Another World in Sky!" Americans were thrilled at the discovery of another planet in space. Walt Disney jumped on the bandwagon and named his cartoon dog Pluto. A new element, plutonium, was named after the new planet.

However, around seventy-five years after its official discovery, Pluto was no longer considered a planet. In August 2006, it was downgraded to dwarf planet by the International Astronomical Union (IAU). The reason was that Pluto did not meet the three major criteria used to define a planet.

According to the IAU, a planet must orbit the Sun, have a shape that is nearly round, and have cleared the area around its orbit. Since Pluto has not met the third criteria, it is considered a dwarf planet, a classification that was adopted in 2006.

Engineering Feats

Throughout the Depression years, a succession of mighty structures was completed all around America. These feats of engineering, which made use of the latest building technologies, were symbols of progress that cheered Americans during their dark days, at least for a while. In New York City, the world's tallest skyscraper—the 102-story, 1,250-foot-high Empire State Building—opened on May 1, 1931, having been built in less than two years.

The building's architect, R. H. Shreve, claimed that although the building weighed 600 million pounds, because of its placement on 220 columns, its impact on the earth beneath it was equal to that of a 45-foot-high pile of rock. The building contained 10 million bricks, 2.5 million feet of electric wire, 50 miles of radiator pipe, 3,500 miles of telephone and telegraph cable, and 67 elevators placed within 7 miles of elevator shaft. The Empire State Building attracted the attention of moviegoers in 1933 when the film *King Kong* showed the giant ape climbing up the outside of the building. Millions of visitors during the 1930s had an uplifting experience riding the Empire State Building's elevators into the sky above Manhattan. Unfortunately, although two million square feet of office space was available, the Empire State Building remained largely vacant for many years because most businesses during the Great Depression could not afford the rent.

Magnificent new bridges were also completed during the 1930s. In New York, the George Washington Bridge (1931) spanned the Hudson River from Manhattan to Fort Lee, New Jersey. It was suspended from great towers of steel and swayed with the wind. The Triborough Bridge system (1936) linked the boroughs of Manhattan, Queens, and the Bronx. On the other side of the country, the eight-mile-long San Francisco–Oakland Bay Bridge (1936) connected San Francisco and Oakland, California. The Golden Gate Bridge (1937) joined San Francisco and the Marin Headlands. More than a quarter of a million

World's Fairs

Americans in the 1930s needed a dose of optimism to help them deal with life during the Depression. That spark of hope came about in the form of several World's Fairs. The largest took place in Chicago and New York.

In 1933 and 1934, the Chicago World's Fair, called The Century of Progress Exposition, focused on the progress in science and technology that had occurred since the founding of Chicago in 1833. More than thirty-nine million visitors were encouraged to view their current economic difficulties from a long-term perspective. The exhibits proved that America's course was onward and upward.

The New York World's Fair of 1939 and 1940 was called The World of Tomorrow. This exposition presented a vision of a fabulous future life of ease and prosperity. Machines, such as Elektro the Talking Robot, would do much of the work. And a fantastic invention called television would allow people to experience faraway sights and sounds in the comfort of their own living rooms. To many Americans, it seemed as though these concepts had been borrowed from the world of Buck Rogers, a science fiction comic strip hero of the time.

people walked across the Golden Gate Bridge on October 1, 1937, the day it opened.

In the Southwest, a huge dam was built on the Colorado River to provide electricity to places, such as Los Angeles, and to control flooding. The construction of the Boulder Dam began in September 1930. The project, finished in 1936, created hundreds of jobs. Unfortunately, many workers died of heat exhaustion under the broiling desert sun. The 725-foot-high Boulder Dam, one of the tallest dams in the world, created 15-mile-long Lake Mead. Because Herbert Hoover, as Secretary of Commerce, played a big role in planning and funding the project, the dam was later officially renamed the Hoover Dam.

Goddard's Experimental Rockets

Robert Hutchings Goddard, an engineer in Massachusetts, began developing experimental rockets in 1915. He had a dream that one day rockets would carry people into space. In 1920, Goddard published his ideas in *A Method of Reaching Extreme Altitudes*. He wrote that rockets could be used to transport a small vehicle to the moon. Of course, such ideas were far ahead of their time. Most people were still getting used to the idea of traveling in automobiles. Not surprisingly, Goddard had to endure a great deal of ridicule. But he was not discouraged. He continued to work on his rockets.

After the local fire chief complained that the rockets might start a fire, Goddard relocated to New Mexico. In December 1930, Goddard launched a rocket powered by liquid oxygen and gasoline. The rocket shot up 2,000 feet into the air at a speed of 500 miles per hour. Five years later, one of Goddard's rockets soared as high as 4,800 feet in the sky. Although the pioneer rocket scientist would not live to see it, his dreams would come true three decades later when astronauts traveled to the moon.

Thirty-six people died when the **Hindenburg** crashed.

Fiery Crash of the *Hindenburg*

For a brief period in the 1930s, it seemed that a new type of passenger transportation had arrived—the rigid airship known as the dirigible or zeppelin, which was named after Count Ferdinand von Zeppelin, the German engineer who developed it. In 1936, the 804-foot-long, hydrogen-filled German airship *Hindenburg* began making flights across the Atlantic Ocean. The length of three jumbo jets placed end-to-end, it could carry as many as fifty passengers and a crew of about fifty in comfort. As the giant airship floated silently across the sky high above the ocean waves, passengers enjoyed an experience comparable to being on a luxury ocean liner. Inside the massive airship was a dining room, a lounge, a smoking room, and private cabins.

The trip from Germany to New Jersey usually took fifty to sixty hours and cost $400 one way or $720 round trip. By May 1937, the *Hindenburg* had made thirty-six trips across the ocean. Plans were being made to build more airships and to begin regular transatlantic flights. But on May 6, 1937, disaster struck. As the *Hindenburg* prepared to land at Lakehurst, New Jersey, the hydrogen inside exploded and the zeppelin burst into flames. Thirty-six people were killed. Sadly, the age of the passenger airship came to a sudden close.

Early Antibiotics

Wonder drugs! That's what people called the new sulfa drugs. Sulfa drugs, or sulfonamides, were the first drugs to fight bacterial infections, such as scarlet fever and meningitis, successfully. In 1932, German biochemist Gerhard Domagk noticed that a red dye known as Prontosil cured certain infections in laboratory mice. Researchers in Paris investigated Prontosil and found that its active ingredient was sulfonamide.

American researchers at Johns Hopkins Hospital did clinical research and found that Prontosil was effective against bacterial organisms, such as streptococcus, meningococcus, and gonococcus. Sulfonamides would later be used as the first antibiotics to fight illnesses that had long plagued people all over the world and save countless lives.

A sample of hemolytic streptococci viewed through a microscope.

Conclusion

The Roaring Twenties had been a time of great prosperity in America, but then came the crash of the New York stock market in the fall of 1929. Suddenly, the party was over. The Great Depression threw millions out of work. To make matters worse, a severe drought made it impossible for many farmers to grow crops. Hundreds of thousands of families were forced to give up their farms. Many headed west to find work and became migrant farmers in California.

The decade of the 1930s was, for many Americans, the most difficult time of their lives. For many people facing the scary prospect of no longer having a job, it was a question of survival. How would they eat? Where would they sleep? Many wondered whether the shattered economy would ever revive. Some people began to think that perhaps the capitalist system itself was in need of replacement.

President Roosevelt ushered in a new era of hope. His New Deal programs helped bring the country through the Great Depression with many new agencies designed to help ordinary people and provide jobs for those who were out of work. Ultimately, it would take World War II in the 1940s, which would be fought to combat fascism in Europe and Asia, to restore the American economy. The war would dominate the events of the next decade. It was the most destructive conflict in human history.

At first, the German and Japanese militaries won great victories. By early 1942, it seemed as though they could not be stopped. However, Americans fought bravely on many battlefields and helped soldiers from Great Britain and the Soviet Union defeat the German army in Europe. They recaptured islands taken by the Japanese. The United

Canadian soldiers in battle gear and gas masks participate in a drill. The conflicts of the 1930s would culminate World War II.

States developed many new weapons, but one was more deadly than the others—the atomic bomb. With a single blast, tens of thousands of people could be killed. Japan finally surrendered after the United States destroyed two of its cities with atomic bombs.

At the start of the 1940s, European countries controlled large overseas empires. But by the time World War II ended in 1945, Europe was left in ruins. The European empires began to break apart. People living in the British and French colonies in Africa, Asia, the Middle East, and South America began to seek independence. New countries were created all over the world.

Although the United States and the Soviet Union had worked together to defeat Germany, the two countries became bitter rivals after the war ended. A conflict known as the Cold War began in the late 1940s. The armed forces of the United States and the Soviet Union did not fight each other directly. Instead, the two superpowers tried to get other countries to support their political and economic systems and prevent the other side from gaining allies. The Cold War would continue until the early 1990s.

Timeline

1930   The decade begins in the midst of the Great Depression after the stock market crash of 1929. On February 18, Clyde Tombaugh photographs the planet that will be known as Pluto. President Hoover promises on March 7 that the Depression will be over in sixty days. On June 17, Hoover signs the Hawley-Smoot Tariff into law. In September, construction begins on Boulder (Hoover) Dam; In

the fall, Hoover creates the President's Emergency Committee for Employment (PECE). *Little Caesar* opens in theaters.

1931   In May, Hoover says allowing the government to provide Depression relief will hurt the character of the American people. *The Public Enemy* premieres in theaters. *Dracula* and *Frankenstein* premiere. The Scottsboro boys are arrested on rape charges. Japan occupies Manchuria. On May 1, the Empire State Building opens in New York City. The George Washington Bridge, linking New York City and New Jersey, opens.

1932   On March 1, the Lindbergh baby is kidnapped. Babe Didrikson wins two gold medals and sets hurdle records in the Olympics. The Bonus Army marches on Washington, D.C., and is met with violence from government forces. German biochemist Gerhard Domagk finds that Prontosil cures infections in lab mice. In November, Franklin D. Roosevelt is elected president.

1933 President Franklin Roosevelt is inaugurated on March 4. Roosevelt sets up the Agricultural Adjustment Administration (AAA). Prohibition is repealed. The Chicago World's Fair begins. *King Kong, 42nd Street, Flying Down to Rio*, and *Duck Soup* premiere in theaters. The Roosevelt administration creates the Federal Deposit Insurance Corporation (FDIC). Japan withdraws from the League of Nations. Adolf Hitler becomes Chancellor of Germany.

1934 Shirley Temple has her first starring role in *Stand Up and Cheer. The Thin Man* premieres. President von Hindenburg dies, and Adolf Hitler assumes complete control over the German government.

1935 Amelia Earhart makes the first flight from Hawaii to California. The Soil Conservation Service (SCS) is established. Bingo is introduced. Monopoly is introduced. The first chain letters appear in the mail. *Mutiny on the Bounty* premieres. The US Supreme Court declares the National Recovery

Administration unconstitutional. Mussolini orders an Italian invasion of Ethiopia. Nuremberg Laws deprive German Jews of many rights.

1936 Bruno Richard Hauptmann is executed for the murder of the Lindbergh baby. Jesse Owens and other African American athletes win eight gold, three silver, and two bronze medals at the Olympic Games in Munich. In July, General Francisco Franco begins the Spanish Civil War when he attempts to overthrow the government. The Triborough Bridge, link-

ing Manhattan, Queens, and the Bronx, opens. In November, Franklin Roosevelt is reelected president. CIO begins a wave of labor strikes. Ethiopian emperor Haile Selassie appeals to the League of Nations to help remove Italian forces from Ethiopia. Hitler's forces occupy the Rhineland. Germany, Italy, and Japan form the Axis Powers.

1937 Amelia Earhart disappears while on a flight around the world. Japan begins war with China. During the fighting in the Spanish Civil War, Hitler's Condor Legion bombs the city of Guernica. The Golden Gate Bridge opens and links San Francisco and Marin County, California. On May 6, the *Hindenburg* explodes over New Jersey.

1938 On March 12, Hitler annexes Austria. Walt Disney releases *Snow White and the Seven Dwarfs*; In September, British Prime Minister Neville Chamberlain and Hitler sign the Munich Agreement. On October 30, Orson Welles's radio broadcast of *The War of the Worlds* leads people to believe Martians have invaded earth. On November 9, the Kristallnacht attack on Jews takes place in Germany and Austria. Hitler takes over Czechoslovakia. Mussolini invades Albania.

1939 *The Grapes of Wrath* is published. The New York World's Fair begins, at which the television is introduced. *My Little Chickadee, Stagecoach, The Wizard of Oz,* and *Gone With the Wind* open in theaters. Billie Holiday records "Strange Fruit." Francisco Franco becomes dictator of Spain. On August 23, Hitler and Stalin sign a nonaggression pact. On September 1, Hitler's troops invade Poland, thereby starting World War II.

Glossary

anti-Semitism—Anti-Jewish sentiment.

appeasement—Giving in.

bootlegging—The sale of illegal alcohol.

chancellor—Title of the top government official in Germany.

cultural pluralism—When a smaller group within a larger society is able to maintain their cultural identity.

dictator—A harsh and controlling ruler.

dirigible—Steerable, lighter-than-air airship.

fascism—System of government that is nationalistic and authoritarian to the extreme.

Hooverville—Shantytowns built by the homeless and destitute during the Great Depression.

improvise—To change, invent, or create without planning.

lynch—To kill someone without the benefit of a legal trial.

resources—Objects from nature that are valuable to humans, such as wood, water, oil, and metals, such as iron.

navigator—A person who plans the course of a ship or aircraft.

propaganda—Information used to sway public opinion that is often false or misleading.

repatriation—Returning a people to their place of origin.

speakeasy—Nightclub or store that sold liquor illegally during the Prohibition.

tariff—A fee paid on goods imported or exported, often used to encourage consumers to buy domestic products.

transient—Person who stays and works in a place for a short time then moves on to a new opportunity.

treason—An act of betrayal against one's country.

Further Reading

Books

Allen, Frederick L. *Since Yesterday: The 1930s in America.* New York: Harper Perennial, 1986.

Deem, James M. *Kristallnacht: The Nazi Terror That Began the Holocaust.* Berkeley Heights, N.J.: Enslow Publishers, 2012.

Duncan, Dayton. *The Dust Bowl: An Illustrated History.* San Francisco, Calif.: Chronicle Books, 2012.

Fremon, David K. *The Great Depression in United States History.* Berkeley Heights, N.J.: Enslow Publishers, 2014.

Goodwin, Doris Kearns. *No Ordinary Time.* New York: Simon & Schuster, 1994.

Lace, William W. *The Hindenburg Disaster of 1937.* New York: Chelsea House Publishers, 2008.

Stone, Tanya Lee. *Amelia Earhart.* New York: DK Books, 2007.

Web Sites

memory.loc.gov/ammem/fsowhome.html

The Library of Congress's resources for the Great Depression to World War II.

xroads.virginia.edu/~1930s/front.html

Become immersed in the decade with this site.

whitehouse.gov/history/presidents/fr32.html

Franklin D. Roosevelt's biography page.

pbs.org/wgbh/amex/rails/

PBS's companion site to its miniseries on the Great Depression, *The American Experience: Riding the Rails*.

Movies

Bonnie and Clyde. Directed by Arthur Penn. Burbank, Calif.: Warner Brothers, 1967.

Stylish love story of the American criminals.

The Grapes of Wrath. Directed by John Ford. Los Angeles, Calif: 20th Century Fox, 1940.

Film adaptation of John Steinbeck's novel depicting Okies and migrant workers.

Index

Federal Music Project, 31
Federal Reserve System, 51
Federal Theatre Project, 31
Fitzgerald, Ella, 34
Franco, Francisco, 66, 69

G

Gable, Clark, 33
Garbo, Greta, 24
Garland, Judy, 33
George Washington Bridge, 77
Goddard, Robert Hutchings, 79
Golden Gate Bridge, 77
Goodman, Benny, 34
Grapes of Wrath, The, 16
Guthrie, Woody, 52

H

Hauptmann, Bruno Richard, 23
Hawes, Elizabeth, 24
Hawley-Smoot Tariff Act, 47
Hemingway, Ernest, 69
Hindenburg, 81
Hirohito, emperor of Japan, 60
Hitler, Adolf, 41, 42, 64, 66, 69, 70,
    71, 72
Holiday, Billie, 34, 36
Holocaust, 71
Hoover Dam, 79
Hoover, Herbert, 7, 8, 9, 11, 15, 47,
    48

I

Indian Reorganization Act of 1934,
    59

J

jigsaw puzzles, 22

K

Karloff, Boris, 31
Kristallnacht, 69

L

Laughton, Charles, 31
League of Nations, 60, 64, 65
Leigh, Vivien, 33
Lewis, John L., 52
Lindbergh baby kidnapping, 21, 23
Lindbergh, Charles, 21, 23, 34
Louis, Joe, 42
Lowell, Percival, 74
Lugosi, Bela, 31

M

Marx brothers, 31
Miller, Glenn, 34
Monopoly, 24
Mussolini, Benito, 64, 66, 72

N

National Association for the
    Advancement of Colored People
    (NAACP), 56
National Industrial Recovery Act
    (NIRA), 51
National Labor Relations Act
    (NLRA), 52
National Recovery Administration
    (NRA), 51

National Youth Administration (NYA), 55
Nazi party, 64, 69, 70
Nelson, "Baby Face", 19
New Deal, 8, 28, 31, 48, 51, 55, 59, 84
New York Yankees, 39
Noonan, Frank, 12
Nuremberg Laws, 69

O

Owens, Jesse, 42

P

Parker, Bonnie, 8, 19, 21
Picasso, Pablo, 69
Pluto, 74, 76
Pollock, Jackson, 31
Powell, William, 31
President's Emergency Committee for Employment (PECE), 9

R

Randolph, A. Philip, 56
Reece, Florence, 51
repatriados, 56
Riefenstahl, Leni, 41
Robinson, Edward G., 31
Rogers, Ginger, 31
Roosevelt, Eleanor, 56
Roosevelt, Franklin Delano, 7, 8, 16, 20, 28, 40, 48, 51, 52, 55, 56, 59, 84
Ruth, George Herman "Babe", 39

S

San Francisco–Oakland Bay Bridge, 77
Selassie, Haile, 64
Shelterbelt Project, 19
Shreve, R. H., 77
Soil Conservation Service (SCS), 16, 19
Spanish Civil War, 66, 69
Stalin, Joseph, 67, 72
Steinbeck, John, 16
sulfa drugs, 81

T

Temple, Shirley, 32
Tennessee Valley Authority (TVA), 51
Tombaugh, Clyde W., 74
Triborough Bridge, 77
Tugwell, Rexford, 48

U

United Mine Workers of America (UMWA), 52

W

Wayne, John, 31
Welles, Orson, 33, 34
White, Walter, 56
Wood, Grant, 31
Works Progress Administration (WPA), 28, 31, 51, 55, 56
World War I, 60, 65, 66, 70, 71
World War II, 47, 63, 72, 84, 86
Wynn, Ed, 33